IRON PEGGY

ALSO BY MARIE CLEMENTS

*Burning Vision**

*Copper Thunderbird**

The Edward Curtis Project: A Modern Picture Story
(with Rita Leisner)*

Talker's Town and The Girl Who Swam Forever
(with Nelson Gray)*

*Tombs of the Vanishing Indian**

*The Unnatural and Accidental Woman**

*Published by Talonbooks

IRON PEGGY

A PLAY

WITH STUDY GUIDE

MARIE CLEMENTS

TALONBOOKS

Talonbooks
9259 Shaughnessy Street, Vancouver, British Columbia, Canada v6p 6r4
talonbooks.com

Talonbooks is located on xʷməθkʷəy̓əm, Sḵwx̱wú7mesh, and səl̓ilwəta?ɬ Lands.

First printing: 2020

Typeset in Arno
Printed and bound in Canada on 100% post-consumer recycled paper

Interior and cover design by Typesmith
Cover illustration by Monique Hurteau

Talonbooks acknowledges the financial support of the Canada Council for the Arts, the Government of Canada through the Canada Book Fund, and the Province of British Columbia through the British Columbia Arts Council and the Book Publishing Tax Credit.

Rights to produce *Iron Peggy*, in whole or in part, in any medium by any group, amateur or professional, are retained by the author. Interested persons are requested to contact Marie Clements, One New Road, Galiano Island, British Columbia, von 1p0; telephone: 778-881-3801.

Iron Peggy was commissioned by the Vancouver International Children's Festival with funds from the Canada Council for the Arts' New Chapter program and the BC Arts Council's Performing Arts Theatre Projects.

LIBRARY AND ARCHIVES CANADA CATALOGUING IN PUBLICATION

Title: Iron peggy / Marie Clements.
Names: Clements, Marie, 1962– author.
Description: A play.
Identifiers: Canadiana 20200182463 | ISBN 9781772012538 (SOFTCOVER)
Classification: LCC PS8555.L435 I76 2020 | DDC C812/.6—dc23

For all the Indigenous soldiers who fought with such bravery in the World Wars and brought this grace and will to the fight for equality in Canada. To those, however young, who are standing their ground with their still minds, steely guts, and open hearts. I thank you all for the courage forward.

PRODUCTION HISTORY

Iron Peggy was first produced from May 28 to 31, 2019, by the Vancouver International Children's Festival and Boca del Lupo in association with Red Diva Projects in Vancouver, British Columbia, with the following cast and crew:

PEG	Adele Noronha
FRANCIS "PEGGY"	
PEGAHMAGABOW	Deneh'Cho Thompson
HENRY LOUIS NORWEST	Raes Calvert
PRIVATE GEORGE MCLEAN	Taran Kootenhayoo
GRANDMOTHER	Balinder Johal

Director	Sherry J. Yoon
Stage Manager	Yvonne Yip
Composer / Cellist	Cris Derksen
Singer	Neeraja Aptikar
Set and Prop Design	Shizuka Kai
Costume Design	Mara Gottler
Video Design	Jay Dodge
Sound Design	Carey Dodge
Lighting Design	Jeff Harrison
Dramaturge	Paula Danckert
Prop Builder	Monica Emme
Fight Choreographer	Jonathan Hawley Purvis
Cultural Consultant	Gavan Cheema
Production Assistant	Kathleen Gordon
Technical Director	Debbie Courchene
Executive Producer	Katharine Carol
Associate Producer	Michelle Kneale

CHARACTERS

PEG, age ten. British Indian. Mixed blood. Her mother was originally from India, and her father is English. A new student at a private girl's school in London. Smart, pretty, and kind. Faced with odds she can't seem to fight against. Must be played by a South Asian actor.

GRANDMOTHER, in her early sixties. Peg's beautiful grand-mother, who writes to her every week from India. She worked hard from a young age and became a designer, securing a better life for her family. Soft-spoken, graceful, and insightful. Must be played by a South Asian actor.

IRON SOLDIER FIGURINES:

Francis **"PEGGY"** Pegahmagabow, age twenty-one. Ojibway. The most decorated military sniper in the Canadian army in World War I. An expert sniper, marksman, and scout. A leader and activist in life, and leader of the **IRON SOLDIER FIGURINES**. Must be played by an Indigenous actor.

HENRY Louis Norwest, age twenty. Cree. A highly decorated famous sniper from World War I. An ex-rodeo performer. Deadly, but with a kind heart. Must be played by an Indigenous actor.

PRIVATE GEORGE McLean, age eighteen. Interior British Columbia Salish. Another highly decorated sniper from World War I. An ex-rancher. A skinny guy with a strong instinct. Must be played by an Indigenous actor.

The actors playing the **IRON SOLDIER FIGURINES** also play:

TWO TEACHERS. Teachers at York Girl's School, one of whom is **MRS. FREED**, aged sixty. An almost-retired teacher.

MS. HALL, age forty-five. The dean of York Girl's School.

IT GIRLS, age thirteen. Three bigger-than-life bullies. Students at the same private girl's school.

ENEMY SOLDIER SHADOWS.

SETTING AND TIME

PLACE: York Private Girl's School, London.

TIME: The present.

SET: A simple set with a backdrop that can construct and create shadows and projection.

SHADOW PLAY AND PROJECTIONS: Where characters are described as shadows they might also be realized by video, depending on strategy.

LIGHTING: Should be able to create hallways and battlefields in the classroom. Dark and light, shadows that become real.

COSTUMES: The costumes for the IRON SOLDIER FIGURINES and for the IT GIRLS and all other characters should be towering above everything else. Exaggerated and bigger-than-life.

NOTE

Slashes (/) indicate run-over dialogue.

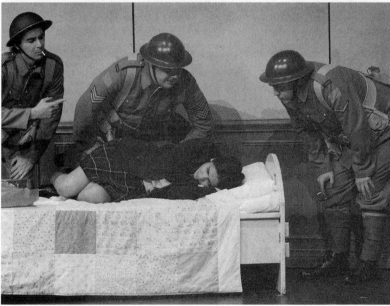

TOP: Adele Noronha in *Iron Peggy*, by Marie Clements, at the Vancouver International Children's Festival, May 28 to 31, 2019. Photo by Farah Nosh.
BOTTOM: Adele Noronha, Taran Kootenhayoo, Deneh'Cho Thompson, and Raes Calvert in *Iron Peggy*. Photo by Farah Nosh.

SCENE ONE: YORK GIRL'S SCHOOL

*Lights up on three TEACHERS at the front of
the stage faced toward the back wall. The tallest is
MS. HALL, who sits in the middle. She is terribly
tall, like a yardstick, and has a big, tight bun in the
centre of her head – from behind, that is. On either
side of her sit two other TEACHERS, who are
round in a kind sort of way, and wearing plaid.*

*A beam of light draws a long hallway down
from the chairs. There at the very end – the
feet of a young girl. Just black shoes.*

MS. HALL
Can you step forward? Please. We can't see you.

Nothing.

MS. HALL
Peg. I'm asking you to step forward so we can see you.

*PEG steps forward and into the light. Her
head is lowered and she is wearing a severely
messed-up York School uniform.*

MS. HALL
Can you raise your head and look at us?

PEG takes a breath and finally looks up.
Her black hair is all over the place, she has a
black eye, and she has clearly been crying.

MS. HALL
Can you tell us who did this to you?

Nothing.

MS. HALL
We can't help you unless you help us.

Nothing.

MS. HALL
Really Peg … you have nothing to say?

PEG just looks at the TEACHERS
and then lowers her eyes.

MS. HALL
You are dismissed, then. Get yourself cleaned up.

PEG
(*softly*) Yes, Ms. Hall.

PEG turns to go and then walks toward them.

PEG
Has my dad sent any word for me?

MS. HALL
He's a very busy man, Peg. I'm sure he'll call, or send a note once
he gets to America. I know you miss him.

PEG tries to smile but she can feel the
tears start to fall. She looks down.

MS. HALL
  Peg?

PEG
  Yes.

MS. HALL
  Your grandmother wrote ... Here it is. Here, come get it.

  PEG moves to the chairs, her eyes down.

MS. HALL
  Chin up. Growing pains. Kids can be cruel, but it rarely lasts.
  New schools get old. You'll see. You'll be fine.

  PEG takes her grandmother's letter from MS. HALL.
  She turns and begins the long walk. She looks
  back – the lights have faded on the TEACHERS.

  PEG is left alone as she makes her way down the
  hall. The walls of the hallway seem to narrow. She
  walks as though anything could come out from either
  side of the darkness – because "they" could be there.
  Each step is painfully taken – are "they" there in
  the darkness or not? PEG's last few steps to safety
  quicken. PEG stops and turns into the next scene.

SCENE TWO: PEG'S DORM ROOM

There is a single bed and a side table, a small desk and chair. The ceiling seems to go up forever. It is old and rich in a bleak, scary sort of way. PEG drags the chair and props it up under the doorknob to make sure nobody can get in from the outside. She sits on the bed, finally relaxing.

PEG smells the letter. It smells like her grandmother – and then suddenly GRANDMOTHER is there, sitting behind her, just to the right of PEG – a SHADOW. PEG reads her grandmother's letter and we hear GRANDMOTHER's voice speaking in Hindi. PEG speaks English as she reads.

GRANDMOTHER	PEG
(*in Hindi*) Beti main tumhare barey main hi soch rahi thi. Aisa lagta hai ki barson beet gaye, tumhara sundar sa chehra dekhe. Tumhari Maa bilkul tumhare jaisi dikhati thi, jab woh tumhari umar ki thi.	Granddaughter, I am thinking of you now. It seems so long since I have seen your beautiful face. You look so much like your mother when she was your age.

GRANDMOTHER laughs like a stream.

GRANDMOTHER
(*in Hindi*) Tumhari ankhein or tumhara saaf dil bilkul tumhari Ma jaisa hai. Kaash ki woh is waqt humaare saath hoti. Lekin hamien himmat banaaye rakni hai.

PEG
Yes. You have her eyes and her good heart. I wish she was with us. But we have to be strong. Yes?

GRANDMOTHER
(*in Hindi*) In garmiyon ki chuttiyon main main shayad tumse milne aaungi. Tumhaara hasmukh chehra dekhane ka bahut mann ho raka hai. Temhaari yeh buddhi naani hawaai jahaajh pe baith ke aayegi. Mujhe pura yakeen hai ki tum apni nayi paathshala main khoob mun laga ke padh rahi hogi or aagey badh rahi hogi. Mai jaanti hun ki tumhare liye apne pariwaar se dur rehna mushkil ho raha hoga. Lekin main tumhien har roz yaad karti hoon or bohot pyaar karti hoon. Tumhari Nani-ma.

PEG
I am thinking I might come and see your funny face this summer. This old grandmother getting on a plane! I know you must be getting really smart at your new school. It must be a shock to be living apart from your family. But I think of you every day and love you as always. Love, your grandmother. Write to me soon.

PEG places the letter on the bed. She goes to the desk and takes out a piece of paper and grabs a pen. She sits back down and begins to write.

PEG
Dear Grandmother, I hate it here. Can you come and get me please? Everybody hates me. Everybody hates me … please come and get me. Grandmother, please. Dad doesn't come visit me. He is gone too. Working. Mom is … dead. Please, Grandmother … please come and get me, please.

PEG begins to cry, finally letting it out.

I can't take it anymore ... There are these girls. Three girls who follow me everywhere. They think they are so smart. They think they are so pretty. So IT. They hate me. They hate me for being me ... Please, Grandmother ... Please come now ... I can't take it anymore. I can't take it anymore ...

> *GRANDMOTHER puts her hand on PEG's shoulder. PEG feels it.*

PEG
Grandmother? Grandmother, please.

> *GRANDMOTHER begins to walk away from PEG. She stops when she thears PEG's voice, and takes out the letter Peg sent her in response and reads it, as PEG gives voice to it.*

PEG
(*in Hindi*) Namaste Nani-Ma. Khat likhne ke liye dhanayavad. Main apko bahut yaad karti hoon. Mera bhi aapse milne ka bahot mun hai. Yahan sab theek hai. Bahut kuch seekhane ko mil raha hai. Meri pathshala bahut achi hai. Aap mujhpar garv mehsoos karoge. Main aapse bahut pyaar karti hoon. P.S. Mujhe garmiyon me aapse milne ka bahut mun ho raha hai. Bahut bahut pyaar. Aapki pouti, Peg.

PEG
Hello Grandmother. Thank you for your letter. I miss you so much. I can't wait to see you. Everything is good here. I am learning a lot. It is a very good school. I will make you proud. I love you. P.S. I can't wait to see you this summer. Love you so much. Love, your granddaughter, Peg.

> *The SHADOW OF GRANDMOTHER puts the letter away with shaking hands – she knows her granddaughter is lying.*

SCENE THREE: UNDER THE DOOR

PEG looks over as three pieces of paper slide under the door. She reaches over and picks the notes up one by one as they are projected above her.

Note One: "You are ugly." PEG reads:

PEG
I am ugly.

She puts the piece of paper in her mouth and swallows it.

Note Two: "You are stupid." PEG reads:

I am stupid.

She puts the piece of paper in her mouth and swallows it.

Note Three: "You are a stupid ugly Paki." PEG reads:

I am a stupid ugly Paki.

PEG puts the last piece of paper in her mouth and tries to swallow it, too. She begins to get sick to her stomach trying to keep it down. PEG spits the pieces of paper out and looks up.

Sometimes words can make you sick. The words that are spoken to you, and the words that you say to yourself. They get inside you and drop inside your stomach like small, hard rocks.

I know what you're thinking. You're thinking how can one small word, or one small rock hurt so much? Everything adds up. Words can add up. They can get so heavy. A small pebble of a word times a hundred is a boulder inside your belly. It feels so heavy you can barely move. You can barely breathe. Have you ever felt that way? I feel that way all the time. All the time. All the time. All the time until I want to scream –

The school bell rings.

SCENE FOUR: THE HALLWAY – MORNING

> PEG *walks down the long hallway with a huge social studies project in her hands. It is her grandmother's village in the South West Delhi district of India. Peg has made it out of popsicle sticks and coloured paper. It is beautiful.* PEG *is careful not to let the sound of the bustling school hallway get near it. There is laughter in the hallway, and* PEG *smiles, thinking this might be a great day after all. She feels something behind her, and then:*

> *Three large* IT GIRL SHADOWS *come from a distance and loom right behind her like a recurring nightmare.*

IT GIRL ONE
What do you have there?

> PEG *doesn't say anything.*

IT GIRL TWO
Some kind of freak town. Nobody wants to see that.

> PEG *protects her project. The* IT GIRLS *get closer to her with every step.*

IT GIRL THREE
Nobody cares where you came from, we just want you to go back. Go back to India, you stupid Paki.

PEG
That doesn't make sense.

IT GIRL THREE
You know what doesn't make sense. You. You don't make sense.

PEG
I was born here.

IT GIRL THREE
You're not white.

IT GIRL TWO
You could live here a hundred years and you'd still be a dirty Paki.

IT GIRL ONE
You're so dirty ... your skin is brown.

IT GIRL TWO
Poo brown.

>   *PEG stops.*

PEG
Stop it. Please. I've never done anything to you.

IT GIRL TWO
You're here, aren't you?

> *The three* IT GIRLS *begin to circle* PEG, *tapping
> her on the shoulder.* PEG *turns, trying to protect
> her school project.* IT GIRL ONE *pulls* PEG's
> *hair.* PEG *turns to grab her hair back.* IT GIRL
> TWO *suddenly spits in* PEG's *face.* PEG *tries
> to wipe it off.* IT GIRL THREE *takes a long
> swipe with her enormous arms and hands and*
> PEG's *school project falls out of her hands.*

Her grandmother's village falls to the ground,
breaking into a few pieces. The IT GIRLS
start to laugh as the school bell rings.

PEG *drops to her knees, trying to pick up the pieces.*

SCENE FIVE: CLASS ROOM

PEG sits by herself. The three IT GIRLS sit behind her – snickering into her ear. MRS. FREED sits at the front with her back to the audience, facing her class.

MRS. FREED
Peg, would you like to present your project to the class?

IT GIRLS
(*mocking*) Piggy, would you like to present your pigpen to the class?

      PEG gets up.

PEG
I'm sorry. I had an accident.

IT GIRLS (ALL)
You *are* an accident.

PEG
I tripped. I tripped and my project fell on the floor and broke.

      PEG tries not to cry.

IT GIRL THREE
(*mocking*) Don't be a crybaby.

MRS. FREED
This is the second time something like this has happened. I'm sorry, but I'm going to have to give you an incomplete mark. Maybe you'll learn to be more careful.

PEG just stands there.

MRS. FREED
Peg, did you hear me?

IT GIRL ONE
Say something.

MRS. FREED
Peg?

PEG
Yes, I'm sorry, Mrs. Freed.

IT GIRL TWO
I'm sorry I'm such a stupid, clumsy, good-for-nothing pig.

PEG finally turns suddenly.

PEG
(*to the IT GIRLS*) Shut up!

MRS. FREED
Peg!!!

PEG turns back to the front.

MRS. FREED
I will not tolerate that kind of language in my class. Please
remove ... your project ... and go to the Dean's office. Again.

> *PEG looks back at the three* IT GIRLS. *They
> are laughing. She leaves the classroom, her
> damaged school project in her hands.*

SCENE SIX: DEAN HALL'S OFFICE

MS. HALL is sitting waiting for PEG, her back to the audience. There is a long, long silence. PEG feels like she is really in trouble.

Finally, softly:

MS. HALL
Peg, you can sit.

PEG keeps standing.

PEG
I didn't mean to swear out loud. I'm sorry.

There is another long, awkward silence.

MS. HALL
I'm sorry Peg, something has come up that concerns you.

Pause. PEG squirms.

MS. HALL
It's not about what happened today in class.

PEG relaxes slightly.

MS. HALL
We received an unfortunate call this morning.

MS. HALL hesitates.

There's no way to say this but to just say it ... There was an earthquake in the village where your grandmother lived.

PEG
No, no ... she's coming to visit me this summer./

MS. HALL
/I'm sorry to say, but she didn't make it.

PEG
/We're planning to spend summer vacation together. /She just wrote me.

MS. HALL
/Peg, I'm so sorry. I wish there was something I could do.

PEG
My father?

MS. HALL
We've been trying to reach him, but he must be travelling on business out of cell range. I am sure he will get back to us and call you when he can./

PEG
/When he can.

> *PEG lets the pieces of her grandmother's*
> *village fall to the floor – they smash and*
> *break into a thousand different pieces.*
>
> *PEG walks down another hallway made of light.*

SCENE SEVEN: THE HALLWAY

PEG walks past large school windows in
the hallway. Outside, there are the shadows
of large, beautiful, blooming trees.

PEG

My mom met my dad here in London on a spring day like this.
They couldn't forget each other, so they married. True love is like
that. They were both English, but my mom was from India. She
came here to go to university.

> *PEG walks and looks out the second window.*
> *The shadow of a perfect family house appears.*

We lived not far from here in a perfect house.

> *PEG traces the house and then walks*
> *to the next window. There she sees her*
> *GRANDMOTHER'S SHADOW sitting,*
> *as huge, beautiful flowers appear around her.*

PEG

My grandmother would come visit every summer and stay for
two months. She had long black hair that smelled like a yellow
primrose flower that only grows in India. She would tell me
stories. She would hold my hand. She would sing to me. She
loved me. She thought ... I was perfect. She would tell me

anything was possible, because she knew impossible things could happen.

*GRANDMOTHER'S SHADOW disappears,
and PEG walks down the lonely hallway.*

SCENE EIGHT: PEG'S ROOM

*PEG drags her chair and puts it under the
doorknob. She digs underneath the bed, comes
out with a tin box, and sits on the bed.*

PEG
She would write me a letter every week. In every letter she sent
me she put a piece of fabric.

> *PEG opens the box and dumps the contents
> out. Letters and more letters spill out,
> and tiny pieces of colourful fabric.*

She used to work in a clothing factory. It was hard, but she
worked her way up. First hauling long tubes of fabric when she
was my age. Then, she began to sew on the machines ... her tiny
fingers trying to miss the big needle coming down. Then cutting
patterns. She became a designer and sent her only daughter to
university in London. My grandmother designed her own life
from scraps, and designed her daughter's life from dreams.

> *PEG picks up the tin box, then pulls a necklace
> out from beneath her shirt. There is a small key
> on it. PEG unlocks the box and looks inside.*

I wish I could put my heart in this tin box. So nothing could hurt
me. I'll close the door tight and lock it shut with this lock.

> *PEG takes the small lock and places
> it back in the loop of the box.*

And this key.

> *PEG takes the key and locks the tin box. She*
> *puts the necklace and key back under her shirt.*

There. My heart is in here. There. Nothing is going to hurt me.
Nothing is going to touch me. You'll see.

> *PEG lies on the floor hugging her grandmother's*
> *letters and the pieces of fabric all around her.*

> *MUSIC: "Grandmother's Lullaby," in Hindi.*

> *PEG closes her eyes and begins to fall asleep.*
> *Shadows of letters fall from the sky all around*
> *her through her grandmother's lullaby.*

SCENE NINE: PEG'S ROOM – NIGHT

> *A knock at the door. Knock and knock.* **PEG** *wakes up on the floor, and through the crack of the door she can see someone's shoes on the other side.*

> *Another knock. Knock. Knock.*

> *She gets closer to the door but doesn't open it. It might be the three It Girls.*

> **PEG** *listens. She hears footsteps walking down the long hall. She moves the chair, opens the door a crack, and peaks out. There, a parcel.*

> **PEG** *takes the parcel inside her room. She closes the door and secures it with the chair.* **PEG** *turns the parcel over and looks at the address.*

PEG
  South West Delhi District. India.

> **PEG** *opens the parcel excitedly. She rips the cardboard box open, and then unfolds a large scrap of fabric – and inside:*

> *Three small iron Canadian soldier figurines. They clank on the floor.*

> **PEG** *picks them up.*

PEG
Who are you?

PEG turns the figurines this way and that.

Why would my grandmother send me these?

*PEG looks at them really closely,
turning them around.*

You're not even English soldiers. You're not even
soldiers from India.

PEG bends in to talk to one.

Hello.

Nothing.

I said, "Hello."

Pause. Nothing.

Stupid!

A knock at the door.

MRS. FREED
(*offstage*) Peg ... I know you're in there.

PEG freezes and says nothing.

MRS. FREED
(*offstage*) There's a call for you. I think it's your father. Isn't that
great? Why don't you come out now and take the call?

Nothing. And then:

PEG
Tell him I don't want to talk with him. Tell him I'm okay, he can go back to work now ... that's all he cares about anyways.

MRS. FREED
Peg?

PEG
Go away.

> PEG *picks up the Canadian soldier figurines and makes them fight. It's not fun.*

PEG
Stupid.

> PEG *throws the figurines against the wall and lies back down on the floor. They land and don't move.* PEG *doesn't move. She doesn't care.*

SCENE TEN: PEG'S ROOM – NIGHT INTO MORNING

PEG is asleep on the floor. The three Canadian soldier figurines are on the floor by the side of the wall. There's a flash of light. And then another. Another.

The three Canadian soldier figurines have become three IRON SOLDIER SHADOWS that are beginning to grow up from the floor. They are huge.

The SHADOWS stand together and then come right out from the wall in giant military uniforms, larger than life, becoming PEGGY, HENRY, and PRIVATE GEORGE. They move closer to PEG, surrounding her, towering above her.

PEGGY
A casualty?

HENRY
Don't look dead to me. Looks like – dead tired. There's a difference.

PEGGY
I get that.

HENRY
Just sayin' what I see.

HENRY looks over at PRIVATE GEORGE.

PEGGY
Anything?

PRIVATE GEORGE
Nothing to add.

HENRY
Cig?

PEGGY
Sure ... what the hell. Pass the time.

> *HENRY takes out three fake cigarettes, lights them
> all in his mouth, and passes one to PEGGY. PEGGY
> takes it. HENRY passes one to PRIVATE GEORGE.
> PRIVATE GEORGE takes it. They all smoke, sort of.*

PRIVATE GEORGE
Trying to quit but there's always tomorrow. They say it's bad for
your health.

PEGGY
Who's they?

PRIVATE GEORGE
Them.

HENRY
There's always them.

PEGGY
You know what's bad for your health?

HENRY
What?

HENRY
Being dead.

> PEGGY, HENRY, and PRIVATE GEORGE
> all start laughing.

PRIVATE GEORGE
That's funny.

HENRY
It'd be really funny if it wasn't true.

PRIVATE GEORGE
That's true.

> PEGGY, HENRY, and PRIVATE GEORGE
> cock their heads and look down at PEG.

PRIVATE GEORGE
What's her story?

PEGGY
Hard to say, really.

HENRY
I think she's tuckered out.

> PRIVATE GEORGE looks around at the mess.

PRIVATE GEORGE
I think she's one messy girl.

HENRY
I'd agree to that.

PRIVATE GEORGE
You want I can try and wake her.

HENRY
    I wouldn't do that. Girls get real mean when you wake them up.

PEGGY
    We got nothing but time. We can wait.

        *PEGGY throws down his fake cigarette and rubs it
        out with his boot. HENRY and PRIVATE GEORGE
        do the same. They stand at ease watching over her.*

PEGGY
    I once waited nine days for someone to move. I thought they
    might be dead. But nope, they were waiting for me to make
    the first move. I knew that. He knew that but moved anyways.
    Sometimes, most times, it's smarter to make the second move.
    If you know what I mean ...

PRIVATE HENRY
    I agree.

HENRY
    Me too, but she don't look like no soldier.

PEGGY
    Never can be too certain.

PRIVATE GEORGE
    She doesn't look like a soldier, but it doesn't mean she doesn't
    have her own battles.

PEGGY
    We all got them.

        PEGGY, HENRY, and PRIVATE GEORGE nod.

HENRY
    I really want to wake her up.

PRIVATE GEORGE
Do it. Just give her a little nudge.

HENRY
You do it. Scared.

PRIVATE GEORGE
Scared of a girl?

HENRY
Damn straight. I'm a smart man. Had three sisters.

> PEGGY *stretches out his boot and*
> *gives* PEG *a bit of a nudge.*

PEG
(*sleepily*) Leave me alone or I'll punch you in the face!

HENRY
See what I mean?

PRIVATE GEORGE
Scary little thing.

> PEGGY *takes his foot again and nudges* PEG. PEG
> *gets up, hands in fists, trying to shake the sleep off.*

PEG
I'm not scared of you!

PRIVATE GEORGE
No need to be scared.

PEGGY
Rub your sleepy eyes.

PEG
You rub your sleepy eyes!

HENRY
He's just sayin' –

PEG
I can hear. I can hear. Stupid It Girl.

> PEG *rubs her eyes and the three*
> *soldiers come into focus.*

HENRY
(*hurt, to* PRIVATE GEORGE) No one's ever called me a girl.

> PEG *starts to back up.*

PEG
Who are you?

> PEGGY, HENRY, *and* PRIVATE GEORGE *don't*
> *move. Then* PEGGY *steps forward officially.*

PEGGY
Sergeant Major Francis Pegahmagabow ... People like to
call me Peggy.

PEG
My name's Peg. Peggy.

PEGGY
Nice to meet you Peg. Peggy.

PEG
Nice to meet *you* Peggy. Peg.

> HENRY *steps forward officially.*

HENRY
My name is not Peg, Peggy, Peg, but Henry Francis Norwest, reporting for duty.

PRIVATE GEORGE follows officially.

PRIVATE GEORGE
Not a Peg, Peggy, Peg, or a Henry Francis Norwest. Private George at your service.

PEG looks up at them, amazed.

PEG
You look ...

HENRY
You can say it ... We look ...

PEG
Indian. You look Indian.

PRIVATE GEORGE
'Cause we are Indians.

PEG
Not my kind of Indian.

HENRY
We've heard that before.

PEG
I didn't mean it in a bad way. My mother's family was from India.

HENRY
My mother's family is from Canada. Cree.

PEGGY
Ojibway.

PRIVATE GEORGE
Salish.

PEG
Why did they call you Indians?

PEGGY
Because an explorer by the name of Christopher Columbus set
out for India and got lost and instead ended up in the Americas.
I think he was embarrassed, so he called us Indians. He was a
confused sort of guy.

HENRY
Like he discovered us.

PRIVATE GEORGE
Lost guys will say anything.

PEG
You're called First Nations, or Native, or Indigenous now.

PRIVATE GEORGE
Whatever they call us. We know who we are.

HENRY
That sounded pretty good. Solid.

PRIVATE GEORGE
Came out better than I thought it would.

PEGGY looks at PEG, her hands still in fists.

PEGGY
You going to hit us?

>   *PEG looks at her fists.*

PEG
  No.

>   *PEG lets her hands unfold.*

HENRY
  That's good.

PRIVATE GEORGE
  'Cause we're on your side.

PEGGY
  You look like you're ready for battle.

>   *PEG doesn't say anything.* **HENRY** *walks around*
>   *the space and looks at the secured door.*

HENRY
  She's got the surroundings secured.

PRIVATE GEORGE
  Copy that.

>   **PRIVATE GEORGE** *walks around* **PEG.**

HENRY
  She's got attitude.

PRIVATE GEORGE
  I can see and hear that. Copy that.

PEGGY
  It's time.

PEGGY, HENRY, and PRIVATE GEORGE
fall in beside PEG in a line. PEGGY looks
at PEG, motioning her to stand straight.

HENRY
(*whispering to PEG*) You always got to stand straight and tall.

PEG stands straight and tall. PEGGY motions
with his fingers for her to look straight ahead.

PRIVATE GEORGE
You always got to look straight ahead. Look it in the
eye. Never down.

PEG looks straight ahead. HENRY nudges her.

HENRY
What do you say?

PEG
Copy that?

PEGGY, HENRY, and PRIVATE GEORGE smile.

PEGGY, HENRY, and PRIVATE GEORGE
Copy that, Miss!

PEGGY, HENRY, and PRIVATE GEORGE move
around the bedroom. They turn the bed on its side so
it becomes a barricade. They turn the desk on its side.

SCENE ELEVEN: THE BATTLEFIELD

PEGGY addresses his troops.

PEGGY
The most important thing is to be still when everything inside you wants to run or scream. You have to calm everything inside you, like this.

> *He motions for HENRY and PRIVATE GEORGE to stand with him. PEG follows in beside them. PEG tries to become super still. She holds her breath.*

PEGGY
Don't hold your breath, that will just make you pass out, which is not good when someone is trying to kill you. Just keep your body still. Breathe, and your mind will follow.

> *PEG looks at PEGGY and breathes the best she can.*

PEGGY
That's right. You got it.

PEG
For how long?

PEGGY
For as long as it takes. The first rule as a sniper is to still everything so you can see clearly.

PEG
What happens when your brain keeps hearing things it shouldn't?

PEGGY
Think about something that is still in your heart. Like the voice of someone you love. Or a song you were taught.

PEG
What song do you hear?

PEGGY
My grandfather raised me when I was young, because my parents died. He taught me this song to keep me strong. Sometimes when I need to steady everything inside for what is to come, I can hear it.

> MUSIC: "Grandfather's Song," in Ojibway.

> PEGGY closes his eyes and he can hear the beat of the drum of his grandfather's song. HENRY and PRIVATE GEORGE begin to sing underneath.

PEGGY
I block everything else out and let the song take over.

> The space darkens, and dust and smoke begin to fill the battlefield. PEGGY opens his eyes, and he is in battle. Behind him ENEMY SOLDIER SHADOWS begin to crawl and walk hunched over toward him.

PEGGY
Once. I was surrounded by the enemy. They were getting so close I could see their breath in the air. My heart was beating. My mind wanted to scream. But then my grandfather's song came out of nowhere. I took in one breath and raised my rifle. Raised my rifle.

*HENRY and PRIVATE GEORGE sing louder
now as PEGGY grabs his rifle and raises it to
shoot, and dodges shadow bullets coming back
at him. The ENEMY SOLDIER SHADOWS
hunker down behind the bed barricade.*

*PEGGY runs straight toward them – the ENEMY
SOLDIER SHADOWS are on the other side of the
bed barricade. PEGGY reaches his hand over to the
other side of the barricade and grabs a sack of bullets.*

PEGGY
I ran into the enemy so I could steal ammunition my company
needed to fight back with. I ran like no bullet could hurt me.
No bullet could touch me. I ran and then ran back.

PEGGY runs back to his troops.

PEGGY
I got the ammunition and gave it to my company. We fought.
We held our ground.

PEGGY looks at PEG.

PEGGY
I was moving but I was still inside. Do you know what I mean?

PEG
I think so. Your mind was still, so you could do what you
needed to do.

PEGGY
Smart girl.

PEG
Were you scared?

PEGGY
(*smiling*) I was scared before I was still.

PEG
After?

PEGGY
I was never scared like that ever again. I figured if I could do
it once, I could do it again and again. I trained myself. Inside.
To still myself. To hear what I needed to hear to give me strength.
And to see what I needed to see to help me survive.

> *PEGGY takes the scope off his rifle and hands it
> to* PEG. *PEG takes it and looks through it, and a
> giant light target projects itself.* PEG *looks at her
> surroundings and the audience with new eyes.*

PEG
I am still, and I can see everything.

TOP: Adele Noronha and Taran Kootenhayoo in *Iron Peggy*, by Marie Clements, at the Vancouver International Children's Festival, May 28 to 31, 2019. Photo by Farah Nosh.
BOTTOM: Taran Kootenhayoo, Raes Calvert, Adele Noronha, and Deneh'Cho Thompson in *Iron Peggy*. Photo by Farah Nosh.

SCENE TWELVE: BATTLEFIELD TWO

*PRIVATE GEORGE walks around
the space thinking out loud.*

PRIVATE GEORGE
You need guts. Good guts.

PEG
Like a big belly?

PRIVATE GEORGE
No, but sorta? I've never had a big belly but I still have
guts. Big guts.

PEG
How can you be skinny and have big guts?

PRIVATE GEORGE
It's complicated. I was just a skinny kid and I found myself
at Vimy Ridge.

PEG
What's that?

PRIVATE GEORGE
It's like a cliff. A ridge. Vimy Ridge. We were trying to climb a
steep cliff against all odds.

PEG
Were you by yourself?

PRIVATE GEORGE
Thousands were there that day. All scared as shi/

PEG
You can get in trouble for swearing.

PRIVATE GEORGE
Point taken. They were poo scared. We were all scared. All together and all alone. You know what I mean.

PEG
I think so.

PRIVATE GEORGE
Sometimes you can be in a group of people, but it's like everyone's paralyzed. They can't believe what they are seeing. They can't do anything to stop it.

PEG
What did you do?

Shadow bullets fly around PRIVATE GEORGE.

PRIVATE GEORGE
At first nothing. I was just like them. The enemy was getting closer. Shooting. Rat. A Tat. Tat. Rat. A Tat. Tat. Like someone talking bad things in your ear. Rat. A Tat. Tat Rat. A Tat. Tat. I look over.

Larges masses of ENEMY SOLDIER
SHADOWS *start coming over the ridge.*

PRIVATE GEORGE
They're surrounding us. I say under my breath. They're surrounding us. Someone's got to do something. Someone's got to do something. Suddenly, I'm doing something. I take one of my pineapples.

PRIVATE GEORGE reaches down to his belt.

PEG
  Pineapples?!

PRIVATE GEORGE
  It's like a small grenade.

PEGGY
  Really?

> *PRIVATE GEORGE takes the small
> pineapple grenade in his hand.*

PRIVATE GEORGE
  I take my pineapple. I need more than one. Give me the
  pineapples!!!

> *The battlefield expands.*

> *PEGGY and HENRY hurl pineapples
> his way as PRIVATE GEORGE catches
> them like a football player, then hurls them
> across enemy lines. They explode.*

> *First pineapple: BOOM.*

> *Second pineapple: BOOM.*

> *Third pineapple: BOOM.*

> *Fourth pineapple: BOOM. BOOM. BOOM. BOOM.*

> *There's lots of smoke. Then HENRY and PEGGY
> and PEG come coughing toward the light.*

HENRY
　Always the drama queen.

PRIVATE GEORGE
　That's how it happened, no sh – no poo … no kiddin'. No kiddin'.

PEG
　Weren't you scared to be the only one who did anything?

PRIVATE GEORGE
　I was and I wasn't. Okay, I was, but sometimes being the only one
　doing anything is all it takes. You have to follow your gut.

PEG
　You need good guts.

PRIVATE GEORGE
　A good gut will get you far. Stick your gut out.

　　　　PEG sticks out her gut and they begin to
　　　　move into a "Good Gut" song and dance.

PEG
　I got good gut.

ALL
　She's got good gut.

PEG
　I got good gut.

ALL
　She got good gut.

PRIVATE GEORGE
  Pineapple this. Pineapple that.

ALL
  Pineapple this. Pineapple that.

PEG
  I got good gut.

SOLDIERS
  Hey, oh ... the girl's got good gut. The girl's got good gut.

ALL
  Pineapple this. Pineapple that. We got good gut.

PRIVATE GEORGE
  Pineapple Poo/

      *PEG slaps him in the stomach and
      PRIVATE GEORGE starts laughing ...*

      They ALL laugh.

      The school bell rings.

      *The THREE SOLDIERS all stop
      laughing and jump to attention.*

PEG
  It's okay. Really. It's just the school bell.

PEGGY
  Sounded like a war raid to me.

PEG

It's just a bell. Really. It's okay. You can relax.

> PEG *moves toward the bed and motions for them to*
> *set it upright. They do. She motions for them to sit on*
> *the bed with her. Everyone but* HENRY *sits down.*

SCENE THIRTEEN: BATTLEFIELD THREE

PEG
You can come sit on the bed too, you know. Next to me,
if you want.

> *HENRY reluctantly sits beside her.*

PEG
You're in the middle.

HENRY
You're in the middle.

PEG
I know. But you'll be in the middle too, 'cause they're on the end.

HENRY
I was born in the middle.

PEG
What do you mean?

HENRY
I was born on the Prairies. Some people say that's the middle of
Canada. I'm Cree.

PEG
What's Cree?

HENRY

It's an Indigenous Nation in …

PEG

… the middle of Canada.

HENRY

Hey, you're good.

PEG

I've always felt like I'm in the middle, too, 'cause I'm mixed.

HENRY

People in the middle can see both sides. Being a good sniper you spend most of your time in no man's land.

PEG

What's that?

HENRY

It's the space between. The side you're on and the side they're on. And you? Us? We're right smack dab in the middle.

PEG

How do you know what side you're on?

HENRY

Do you know what good is?

PEG

Yes.

HENRY

Then that's the side you're on.

PEG

Maybe the enemy thinks they're good too.

HENRY
Maybe.

PEG
How do you know who is right?

HENRY
Do you know your heart?

PEG doesn't answer.

HENRY
Locked it up, didn't you?

PEG
How'd you know?

HENRY
'Cause I can see everything. I'm a sniper. I can see for miles both ways and back again.

PEG
It wasn't doing me any good.

HENRY
Really? 'Cause it hurt?

PEG
Maybe.

HENRY
Maybe. Hmmm ... So how you gonna live now with no heart? You won't know what is good or right. Maybe you'll end up just like them. Or worse.

PEG
I don't want to talk about it.

HENRY
Sure you do.

PEG
No, I don't.

HENRY
Sure you do.

PEG
I said I don't.

HENRY
Thing I learned is: This here lets you know what side you're on.
Do you know how to be kind?

PEG doesn't look at him.

PEG
What's that got to do with anything?

HENRY
A kind person is on the right side. They can see when someone is
struggling and just needs a helping hand, or just needs a friend.
A kind person is the strongest person I know. If you close your
heart you won't be able to be you.

PEG pretends she's not listening.

PEG
Nobody likes me, anyways.

HENRY
That's not true.

PEG
Yes, it is. You don't know what it's like.

HENRY
You and me, we're in no man's land. We're in the middle and sometimes it feels like we're all alone. There's the side over there ... See, right there ...

The battlefield expands.

PEG looks over and sees two ENEMY SOLDIER SHADOWS hide under the desk barricade. They have their rifles out.

HENRY
And see over there?

PEG looks on the other side, where two SOLDIER SHADOWS are hurt and close to dying, trying to hide under sand bags.

HENRY moves to the middle, in-between everything. He points to the enemy getting ready to shoot and kill the fallen soldiers.

HENRY
That side wants yout to believe that anybody who looks different than them, speaks different than them, believes in things that are different than them, are bad.

PEG
That's not fair.

HENRY
It's not fair. But you don't have a heart, so what do you care?

PEG
I/

HENRY
You can't fight unless you have a heart.

PEG
I'm not a soldier.

HENRY
Yes, you are.

PEG
No, I'm not.

HENRY
Do you believe everyone is equal? That we all feel things? That
we all want the same thing? We all want to be treated well?

PEG
Yes.

HENRY
Then you are a soldier. It is your right to be kind, to be good,
to look after other people who can't look after themselves. It's
your right to use ...

    HENRY points to his heart.

PEG
How do I do that?

HENRY
By opening your heart.

PEG
I'm scared.

HENRY
This world can be scary. War is scary. But do you want to know what's scarier? Not using your heart ...

HENRY sits back down and is so sad he begins to cry.

PEG
Are you okay?

HENRY
Sometimes I get emotional. Sad.

PEG sits down beside him.

PEG
Me too.

HENRY
That's all right ... we all get sad.

HENRY crys a bit more. PEG takes a small hankie out of her suit jacket and dabs his tears.

PEG
You're gonna make me cry.

HENRY
No, you're making me cry.

PEG
I am not.

HENRY
Are too.

PEG and HENRY both cry. PEGGY and
PRIVATE GEORGE hand them their hankies.

PRIVATE GEORGE
It's a little dirty.

HENRY
Gross.

PRIVATE GEORGE
It's not my fault I have active nostrils.

HENRY and PEGGY look at his face
and start to laugh. Then they look at their
crybaby faces and laugh harder.

HENRY
You're funny.

PEG
You're weird.

HENRY stands up and looks over the battlefield.
It has now become a field of white crosses. PEGGY
and PRIVATE GEORGE stand at attention.

PEG gets up and begins to move between the
rows of white crosses, and as she does they
start to bend and become long stems of poppies
that begin to bloom and rise up to the sky.

They are now a field of beautiful
poppies swaying in the wind.

HENRY
We went to war. So you could live. We fought so you could be
who you are.

PRIVATE GEORGE
We all have to fight to make things better every day.

PEGGY
Peg, you have to fight to make things better for yourself. Then
you can fight to make things better for someone else.

> *PEG looks back at him.*

PEG
They're going to come for me.

> *The war heroes PEGGY, HENRY, and*
> *PRIVATE GEORGE move in beside PEG.*
> *They begin to march in a "Marching Song."*

ALL
Still you mind. Steel your gut. Open your heart. Still your mind.
Steel you gut. Open your heart. Still your mind. Steel your gut.
Open your heart.

> *PEG gets totally into it, not realizing she*
> *is suddenly the only one marching.*

PEG
Still you mind. Steel you gut. Open your heart. Still your mind.
Steel your gut. Open your heart.

> *PEG stops and slowly realizes she is alone again. Her*
> *room is empty. She looks around on the floor and*
> *finds the soldiers are now three soldier figurines.*

> *She bends down to them and affectionately*
> *puts them in her hand and whispers:*

PEG

I think my grandmother sent you to me because, maybe, her
grandmother sent them to her when she was young and needed
help ... Did they know you weren't warriors from India? Did
they know you were Indigenous warriors from Canada? I don't
know ... A warrior is a warrior.

*Just then the three IT GIRLS tower
over her, bigger than ever.*

PEG
(*looking up*) Shiiiit.

TOP: Taran Kootenhayoo, Raes Calvert, and Deneh'Cho Thompson in *Iron Peggy*, by Marie Clements, at the Vancouver International Children's Festival, May 28 to 31, 2019. Photo by Farah Nosh.

BOTTOM: Deneh'Cho Thompson, Taran Kootenhayoo, Adele Noronha, and Raes Calvert in *Iron Peggy*. Photo by Farah Nosh.

SCENE FOURTEEN: THE BATTLE OF ALL BATTLES

PEG closes her eyes, and her hands ball into fists as the three IT GIRLS get closer and closer throughout this scene. They are trying to get right inside her head.

IT GIRLS
Nobody feels sorry for you. I would die too if you were my granddaughter. It looks like you've been dragged through the mud. Oh, right. You're a dirty Paki ... that's how your skin is supposed to look. Where's your big important Dad? He didn't even come visit you ... that shows how much he loves you ...

PEG keeps her eyes closed, but you can clearly see that she wants to cry and run, or both.

PEG
Be still. Be still. Be still. Be still.

PEG begins to sing under her breath, and then she hears her GRANDMOTHER's voice join hers.

MUSIC: "Grandmother's Lullaby," in Hindi.

As the three IT GIRLS get closer, PEG can barely hear them. Their lips are moving but she can't hear a word they are saying. Their words whiz by her like bullets.

PEG smiles, remembering the battles.

IT GIRL ONE
Why are you smiling?

IT GIRL TWO
She's crazy.

IT GIRL THREE
Why are you smiling? We're going to hurt you.

  PEG begins to run.

IT GIRL ONE
Look she's running. We got her now.

PEG
(*calling out*) Pineapple One!

IT GIRL TWO
What's this got to do with fruit? I hate pineapple. Too sour.
It hurts my mouth.

  PEG runs and there it is – a giant pineapple sailing
  through the open space. PEG runs and catches it.
  She runs with it and then hurls it close to the feet
  of IT GIRL THREE. The pineapple explodes.

  IT GIRL THREE runs.

IT GIRL THREE
Exploding pineapples! Exploding pineapples! Run!

PEG
(*calling out*) Pineapple Two!

Another giant pineapple sails across the
battlefield. PEG *catches it and hurls it near*
IT GIRL TWO. IT GIRL TWO *can see it*
coming toward her and begins to cry.

IT GIRL TWO
 I hate pineapples! I hate pineapples! I hate them! I hate them!

 The pineapple explodes. There is a huge gust of
 smoke. It clears. IT GIRL TWO *has pineapple*
 running down her face. She is full-on crying.

IT GIRL TWO
Yuck … Yuck … You're mean! You're so mean!

 Now it's just PEG *and* IT GIRL
 THREE. *They face off.*

IT GIRL THREE
No tropical fruit is going to scare me. I love pineapple; I can eat it
all day. Bring it on.

PEG
(*calling out*) Pineapple Three!

 IT GIRL THREE *begins to circle* PEG, *getting closer.*

PEG
Pineapple Three!!!

IT GIRL THREE
Running out of pineapples, are you? Now what are you gonna
do? Try an apple. Maybe an orange. Wooo … scary.

PEG
Pineapple Three!!!!

Pause.

Pineapple Three hurls up into the space. PEG
goes to catch it, and IT GIRL THREE *tries to*
block it. Pineapple Three travels across the space
and hits smack dab into IT GIRL THREE's
back. But it doesn't roll off – it sticks.

IT GIRL THREE *tries to get it off, but the points*
on the pineapple are stuck deep into the back of
her jacket. She can't reach it and begins to panic.

IT GIRL THREE *begins to run around*
the space desperately trying to reach
the pineapple and take it off.

IT GIRL THREE
Get it off me! Get it off me! It's freaking me out!

PEG *watches as* IT GIRL THREE *falls on the*
floor wrestling with the pineapple on her back.
IT GIRL THREE *calls out to her friends.*

IT GIRL THREE
Don't just stand there, stupid! Help me get it off my back!

IT GIRL ONE
It's just a pineapple.

IT GIRL THREE
It's not just a pineapple! It's a mad pineapple! It's a possessed
pineapple!!! Help me!

IT GIRL ONE *and* IT GIRL TWO *come*
to her rescue, but IT GIRL THREE *is*
so freaked out they can't seem to get the
pineapple off. They tug at it and fall.

IT GIRL ONE
　Oaooo … it's a mean pineapple!

　　　IT GIRL ONE holds IT GIRL THREE, and
　　　IT GIRL TWO tries to hold the pineapple.

IT GIRL TWO
　Ouch … Ouch! It's biting me!

IT GIRL THREE
　It doesn't have teeth, stupid.

IT GIRL TWO
　It feels like it! Look!

　　　IT GIRL TWO shows IT GIRL THREE her
　　　hands. Big pointy sticks from the pineapple
　　　are stuck in her hand. She pulls them out.

IT GIRL TWO
　Ouch … Ouch … Ouch …

　　　IT GIRL ONE throws IT GIRL
　　　TWO her handkerchief.

IT GIRL ONE
　Don't be a baby. Wrap it around the pineapple's head.

　　　IT GIRL TWO begins to and then backs away.

IT GIRL TWO
　It's looking at me.

IT GIRL THREE
　It doesn't have eyes.

IT GIRL TWO
    If you say so.

> IT GIRL ONE *walks over, grabs the*
> *handkerchief from* IT GIRL TWO'*s hands,*
> *and drapes it over the pineapple.*

IT GIRL ONE
    Nighty-night.

> *She looks at* IT GIRL TWO.

IT GIRL ONE
    Now pull.

> IT GIRL TWO *grabs the pineapple.* IT GIRL
> ONE *grabs* IT GIRL THREE *and they pull. And*
> *they pull. And they pull. It's a mighty battle.*
>
> *They pull so hard that when the pineapple*
> *rips off* IT GIRL THREE'*s back they fall*
> *backwards.* BOOM. *Like an explosion.*
>
> *The three* IT GIRLS *land in an exaggerated*
> *position … slowly, they crawl back together.*
> *Slowly, they get up and dust themselves off*
> *from the battle. There is dust everywhere.*
>
> IT GIRL TWO *holds the pineapple in her hand*
> *like a winning football. The three* IT GIRLS *look*
> *at each and then look at* PEG *standing all alone.*

IT GIRL THREE
    Who's laughing now? We're gonna kick your ass.

> *The three* IT GIRLS *begin to walk like*
> *victors in a major battle toward* PEG.

PEG

Still you mind. Steel you gut. Open your heart. Still your mind.
Steel your gut. Open your heart.

The three IT GIRLS get closer and bigger.

PEG

Still you mind. Steel you gut. Open your heart. Still your mind.
Steel your gut. Open your heart.

The three IT GIRLS get closer and bigger.

PEG

Still you mind. Steel you gut. Open your heart. Still your mind.
Steel your gut. Open your heart.

IT GIRL THREE

Not so smart, are you? There's three of us and one of you.

PEG

I'm not scared of you.

IT GIRL THREE

That's because you're stupid.

IT GIRL ONE

Dumb. I'd be scared of us if I was you.

IT GIRL TWO.

Yeah.

IT GIRL TWO gets worked up with power.

IT GIRL THREE

You're gonna pay.

IT GIRL TWO
Yeah! Pay big.

IT GIRL TWO
Yeah! Big.

IT GIRL THREE
Why aren't you scared?

IT GIRL ONE
Yeah. You should be scared.

IT GIRL TWO.
Yeah. Real scared.

PEG
Still you mind. Steel you gut. Open your heart. Still your mind.
Steel your gut. Open your heart.

IT GIRL ONE
Is that like a poem?

IT GIRL TWO
Yeah. A poem.

IT GIRL THREE
We don't like poems. Do we, girls?

IT GIRL ONE
We don't like poems.

IT GIRL TWO
Yeah. We don't like poems. I mean, some poems are cool.

*IT GIRL ONE and IT GIRL THREE
look at IT GIRL TWO.*

IT GIRL TWO
But mostly they suck. Yeah.

> *IT GIRL THREE steps closer to PEG.*
> *She leans right in. IT GIRL ONE and*
> *IT GIRL TWO begin to chant:*

IT GIRLS ONE and TWO
Fight! Fight! Fight!

> *PEG begins to chant:*

PEGGY
Still you mind. Steel you gut. Open your heart. Still your mind.
Steel your gut. Open your heart.

> *PEG reaches into her jacket pocket and takes*
> *out the three soldier figurines. IT GIRL ONE*
> *roughly grabs PEG's hand and forces it open.*

IT GIRL ONE
What do you have there?

> *The three IT GIRLS look down into PEG's palms.*

IT GIRL TWO
Looks like little dolls.

PEG
They are soldiers. Indigenous soldiers.

IT GIRL THREE
They're nothing, just like you.

PEG
You don't know who you're messing with.

IT GIRL THREE
Is that right?

IT GIRLS ONE and TWO
Fight! Fight! Fight!

> IT GIRL THREE pushes PEG and swats her hand,
> and the three soldier figurines fall to the ground.

IT GIRLS ONE and TWO
Fight! Fight! Fight!

> IT GIRL THREE looks over at IT GIRL ONE,
> who grabs PEG by the hair and holds her.

PEG
Still you mind. Steel you gut. Open your heart. Still your mind.
Steel your gut. Open your heart.

> From behind the three soldier figurines
> begin to get bigger, becoming larger and
> larger SOLDIER SHADOWS.

IT GIRL THREE
Say that again and I'll punch you.

SOLDIER SHADOWS
(*from behind*) Still you mind. Steel you gut. Open your heart.
Still your mind. Steel your gut. Open your heart.

> IT GIRL TWO nudges IT GIRL THREE.

IT GIRL TWO
I hear something. It's like a giant poem coming. Freakin' scary.

SOLDIER SHADOWS
(*from behind*) Still you mind. Steel you gut. Open your heart.
Still your mind. Steel your gut. Open your heart.

> *IT GIRL TWO looks up.*

IT GIRL TWO
Holy sh –

> *Just then, IT GIRL THREE goes to punch
> PEG. PEG dodges it as three pineapples are
> thrown at the three IT GIRLS. The pineapples
> fly through space in slow motion. They land
> right in the hair of the three IT GIRLS.*

> *The three IT GIRLS begin to run around
> the space like crazy girls trying to get the
> pineapples from their hair, screaming:*

IT GIRLS
My hair! My hair! Not my hair ... please not my HAAIIIRR ...

> *PEG looks up at the three SOLDIER
> SHADOWS as the IT GIRLS disappear. She
> gets in line with them, taking the lead. They
> stand in one place, marching behind her.*

SOLDIER SHADOWS and PEG
Still you mind. Steel you gut. Open your heart. Still your mind.
Steel your gut. Open your heart.

> *The SOLDIER SHADOWS get smaller behind PEG.*

SOLDIER SHADOWS and PEG
Still you mind. Steel you gut. Open your heart. Still your mind.
Steel your gut. Open your heart.

The SOLDIER SHADOWS get
even smaller behind PEG.

SOLDIER SHADOWS and PEG
Still you mind. Steel you gut. Open your heart. Still your mind.
Steel your gut. Open your heart.

    The SOLDIER SHADOWS are gone.

    PEG reaches down to the ground and
    picks up the three soldier figurines.

PEG
Thank you.

    PEG stands before the audience. Her hand reaches
    up, and she takes Peggy's scope out of her suit pocket.

    She raises it to her eye and a projected circle
    of light encircles the whole audience.

PEG
I see you. I see you so clearly. I see you. You are beautiful. You are
smart. You are kind.

    PEG looks at the three soldier figurines in her hand.

PEG
They fought so we could be who we are meant to be. We have
to stand up for who we are, and for those that came before
us. We have to stand up for each other. It's something worth
fighting for.

    Just then, over the PA system:

MS. HALL
(*voice-over*) Would Ms. Peg Chopra-Davis please report
to my office.

> *PEG looks up at the voice and then at the audience.*

PEG
My name is Peg, but you can call me Iron Peggy.

> *Lights out.*

> *THE END.*

IRON PEGGY STUDY GUIDE

Adapted from the guide produced by the Vancouver
International Children's Festival, 2018. Reprinted with
permission of the Vancouver International Children's Festival
Society and Diana Stewart-Imbert.

Deneh'Cho Thompson, Adele Noronha, and Taran Kootenhayoo in *Iron
Peggy*, by Marie Clements, at the Vancouver International Children's
Festival, May 28 to 31, 2019. Photo by Farah Nosh.

BACKGROUND INFORMATION

INDIGENOUS CHARACTERS

Francis "Peggy" Pegahmagabow

Francis Pegahmagabow, Anishnaabe (Ojibway) Chief, war hero, and later vocal advocate for Indigenous Rights and self-determination, was the most decorated Indigenous soldier enlisted with the 23rd Regiment, part of the 1st Canadian Division.

He fought in France and Belgium, where his first real taste of battle came at the second battle of Ypres. Peggy was a skilled marksman. Although no official records were kept, he is often called the most successful allied sniper of the war, credited with killing dozens of German soldiers. Peggy was injured during the Battle of the Somme, shot in the left leg. This injury could have served as his ticket home, but he rejoined his unit as soon as he was able.

One of the twenty-nine members of the Canadian Expeditionary Force to be honoured, Francis fought throughout the entire war and, despite the odds, survived. In recognition of his bravery he earned the military medal and two bars. He was also awarded a 1914–15 Star, the British War Medal, and the Victory Medal.

In the play, Francis "Peggy" Pegahmagabow is twenty-one years old, of Ojibway descent, and a leader of the Iron Soldier Figurines.

More info: www.thecanadianencyclopedia.ca/en/article/francis-pegahmagabow

Henry Louis Norwest

Henry Norwest, Cree, born in northern Alberta, became the greatest sniper among the Canadian troops at the front and possibly the best in the British forces. Norwest was officially credited with 115 observed hits, the record at the time. His reputation was known to the German troops, and they feared him.

Norwest had enormous patience and perseverance. Using a rifle fitted with a telescopic lens, he would wait for days in no man's land to catch his man and never fired unless he was sure he couldn't be seen by the enemy. Norwest was awarded the military medal during the Battle of Vimy Ridge in 1917, and three months later a bar was added to his medal.

On August 18, 1918, less than three months before the end of the war, his luck gave out and he died after being shot by a German marksman.

In the play, Henry Norwest is twenty years old, and of Cree descent. A highly decorated famous sniper from World War I. An ex-rodeo performer. Deadly but with a kind heart.

More info: www.biographi.ca/en/bio/norwest_henry_14E.html; youtu.be/Nx7N2Q9-ZPw

Private George McLean

George McLean's mother, Angele, was the daughter of Johnny Chillihetza, Chief of the Douglas Lake Indian Band, and the niece of N'kwala (Nicola), Grand Chief of the Syilx (Okanagan) people and Chief of the Nicola Valley peoples.

McLean first served during the Boer War (1899–1902) in South Africa. After that war he became a rancher in the Douglas Lake area of B.C. When World War I was declared he volunteered, although he was forty-one years old. McLean is a memorable soldier because he launched a solo attack on a large number of German soldiers (using Mills bombs – small grenades nicknamed "pineapples") at the Battle of Vimy Ridge. McLean earned the distinguished conduct medal, which was the second-highest award for gallantry.

In the play, George McLean is eighteen years old, and of Salish descent from the B.C. Interior. He is another decorated sniper from World War I. An ex-rancher. A skinny guy with a strong instinct.

More info: www.veterans.gc.ca/eng/remembrance/those-who-served /indigenous-veterans/native-soldiers/twowars

WHERE DO THE IRON SOLDIERS IN
IRON PEGGY COME FROM?

Ojibway (Soldier Francis "Peggy" Pegahmagabow)

"The Ojibway (also Ojibwa, Ojibwe and Chippewa) are an Indigenous People in Canada and the United States who are part of a larger cultural group known as the Anishinaabeg."

More info: www.thecanadianencyclopedia.ca/en/article/ojibwa

Interior Salish (Soldier Private George McLean)

"Interior Salish is comprised of the Lillooet, Shuswap (now Secwépemc), Thompson (now Nlaka'pamux), and Syilx/Okanagan First Nations. They are the four First Nation in the interior of British Columbia (although Okanagan territory extends into Washington State) who speak languages belonging to the Interior Salish division of the Salishan language family."

More info: www.thecanadianencyclopedia.ca/en/article/interior -salish-first-nations

Cree

Cree (Soldier Henry Louis Norwest)

"The Cree (Nehiyawak in the Cree language) are the most ... populous Indigenous Peoples in Canada."

More info: www.thecanadianencyclopedia.ca/en/article/cree

For more information about Indigenous languages and Territories, see native-land.ca and indigenouspeoplesatlasofcanada.ca.

DEFINITIONS OF IMPORTANCE

Aboriginal: "Aboriginal" became a popular term after 1982, when section 35 of the Canadian Constitution defined "Aboriginal" as the First Peoples of Canada, including First Nations, Métis, and Inuit Peoples.

First Nations: "First Nations" does not have a legal definition, but it has been popular practice since the 1970s to use this term instead of "Indian," which is now often considered derogatory. "First Nations" does not encompass Métis or Inuit Peoples. "First Nation" (singular) can also refer to a band, a reserve-based community, or a larger tribal grouping and the status Indians who live in them.

Indian: In Canada, "Indian" is the legal term that refers to an Indigenous person who is registered as such under the Indian Act. Non-Indigenous people should generally avoid using the term, as it's now considered derogatory and outdated. (from s3.amazonaws.com/beacon .cnd/66ebd0d0d470fbaf.pdf?t=1540602454)

In India: People or things related to India.

In Britain: British people of Indian origin (from India).

Indigenous: "Indigenous" encompasses a wide range of Aboriginal Peoples and is typically used in international contexts (most notably the United Nations). This study guide uses the term extensively to refer to Aboriginal Peoples in Canada.

Colonialism: "Colonialism" describes the settlement of places like India, Australia, North America, Algeria, New Zealand, and Brazil, which were all controlled by Europeans. In colonialism, one can see great movement of people to the new territory, where they live as permanent settlers, but still maintain allegiance to their mother country. British colonialism in India ended in 1947. More info: www.thoughtco.com/the-british-raj-in-india-195275.

Settler colonialism and **assimilation:** The term "settler colonialism" refers to an ongoing process of destroying one society for the purpose of replacing it with another. To justify this, the Indigenous Peoples are perceived as inferior in contrast to the colonizing group, and thus deserving of what happens to them.

Canada was founded on settler colonialism, and this process of erasure was done first through force – outright genocide – and later through more subtle strategies of containment, such as law (the Indian Act) and residential schools. Settler colonialism continues today, as Canada's Indian Act, though it has been amended many times since its inception, has largely maintained its original form.

Truth and Reconciliation: A Truth Commission or Truth and Reconciliation Commission is a commission tasked with discovering and revealing past wrongdoing by a government (or, depending on the circumstances, non-state actors also), in the hope of resolving conflict left over from the past. In Canada, its mandate is to inform all Canadians about what happened in residential schools. The Commission has documented the truths of Survivors, families, communities, and anyone personally affected by the residential school experience. More info: caid.ca/TRCFinExeSum2015.pdf.

Slur: A slur is an insult intended to inflict emotional pain. Slurs can be used as a way of homogenizing and isolating people along racial or ethnic lines.

In the play, "Paki" is used as a slur by the It-Girls against Peg. This slur's origins can be connected to India's partition and decolonization after independence from Britain in 1947 (which is why it is probably still used mostly in the UK). India and Pakistan have been at war (and still are in the state of Kashmir) since Independence in 1947. More info: en.wikipedia.org/wiki/Paki_(slur).

BULLYING

(from Vancouver School Board District Links)

Students and parents expect schools to be safe places where students can learn and teachers can teach in a warm and welcoming place, free from bullying, intolerance, and violence.

Bullying is a pattern of aggressive behaviour meant to hurt or cause discomfort to another person. Bullies always have more power than victims. Their power comes from physical size, strength, status, and support within the peer group.

Deneh'Cho Thompson, Taran Kootenhayoo, Adele Noronha, and Raes Calvert in *Iron Peggy*. Photo by Farah Nosh.

There are three types of bullying:

- **Physical**: where a person is harmed or their property is damaged
- **Verbal**: where a person's feelings are hurt through insults and name-calling
- **Social**: where a person is shunned or excluded from groups and events

British Columbia Report Bullying Link: erasereportit.gov.bc.ca/.

OVERVIEW OF WORLD WAR I

World War I, often called the "War to end all Wars," was a major conflict from 1914 to 1918 fought between the Allied and Central powers. The main Allied powers were Serbia, France, Russia, and Britain. Americans joined the Allies later in the war, in April 1917. The Central powers were Germany, Austria-Hungary, the Ottoman Empire, and Bulgaria.

The assassination of Austrian archduke Franz Ferdinand on June 28, 1914, by Serb nationalist Gavrilo Princip led to a quick succession of retaliations: Austria declared war on Serbia, followed by Russia protecting its Serbian ally and Germany declaring war on Russia to protect Austria. Subsequently, France declared war on Germany to protect Russia, Germany invaded Belgium to gain access to France, and Britain retaliated by declaring war on Germany. The fighting ended on November 11, 1918 in a general armistice. The war itself officially ended with Germany and the Allies signing the Treaty of Versailles.

CANADA'S INVOLVEMENT

Troops from Canada played a prominent role in World War I. Canada was part of the British Empire in 1914, so when Great Britain declared war on Germany on August 4, 1914, Canada was automatically at war. The next day, due to the overwhelming support of Canadian citizens, the Canadian Governor General officially declared war on Germany.

Because the British Empire extended across the world, this was truly a global war. Along with citizens of other nations in the Empire, such as Australia and India, tens of thousands of Canadians joined the army in the first few months of the war, and more than four thousand Indigenous soldiers signed up. Along with so many other men, they had to endure the hardships of trench warfare and face the dangers of modern weaponry. For a nation of eight million people, Canada's war effort was remarkable. More than 650,000 men and women from Canada and Newfoundland served – over 66,000 died and more than 172,000 were wounded. It was this immense sacrifice that lead to Canada's separate signature on the Treaty of Versailles. No longer viewed as just a colony of England, Canada was truly on the road to standing on its own. It became a founding member of the League of Nations in 1919.

SOME FACTS ABOUT THE WAR

1. The terrorist group responsible for assassinating Archduke Ferdinand was known as the **Black Hand.**

2. More than **sixty-five million men** fought in the war.

3. **Women served in non-combat roles** such as nurses and ambulance drivers, and many women were recruited to fill jobs at home vacated by men who had left to fight, as well as new jobs created as part of the war effort.

4. Russia had the largest **number of casualties (9,150,000),** followed by Germany (7,142,558), Austria-Hungary (7,020,000), and France (6,160,800).

5. WWI marked the first large-scale use of **chemical weapons.**

6. It was the first major war where **airplanes and tanks** were used. When the British first invented tanks they called them "land-ships."

7. In 1917, for the first time, **a human voice was transmitted by radio** from a plane in flight to an operator on the ground – the birth of air traffic control.

8. Famed scientist **Marie Curie** helped to equip vans with X-ray machines that enabled French doctors to see bullets in wounded men. These vans were called "petites Curies," meaning "little Curies."

9. The "**Thomas splint**" was designed to stabilize fractures of the thigh bones in order to move the patient out of the battlefield without causing him pain or further injury. Thighbone injuries went from 80 percent fatality to 80 percent survival between 1914 and 1916.

10. Dogs were used in the trenches to carry messages. A **well-trained messenger dog** was considered a very fast and reliable way to carry messages.

11. **Mills bombs** were small grenades nicknamed "pineapples."

12. Seventy percent of **Canadian men who enlisted** were recent British immigrants, even though they only represented 11 percent of the population. Enlistment rates of Anglo-Saxon Canadians who had been in Canada for several generations and in French Canadian communities were much lower.

13. First Nations and Canadians of African and Asian ancestries **faced discrimination** when trying to enlist and sometimes had to go to a different province to sign up.

14. More than 2,800 **Canadian Nursing Sisters** served in the Canadian Army Medical Corps.

15. Raymond Collishaw, Billy Bishop, and Billy Barker were among WWI's Canadian "**great aces**," military aviators credited with shooting down five or more enemy aircrafts during aerial combat.

More info:

- www.warmuseum.ca/firstworldwar/history/life-at-the-front/trench-conditions/shellshock/

- www.thestar.com/news/canada/2014/08/09/wwi_racism_black_asian_and_aboriginal_volunteers_faced_discrimination.html

- www.omnitv.ca/on/southasian/videos/1971662261001/

THE WAR & INDIGENOUS PEOPLES IN CANADA

OVERVIEW

During World War I, thousands of Indigenous people voluntarily enlisted in the Canadian military. As only those with official "status" were recorded by the Canadian Expeditionary Force (CEF), precise enlistment numbers are unknown. However, it is estimated that over four thousand Indigenous people served.

Indigenous soldiers served in units with other Canadians throughout the CEF in every major theatre of the war and in all the major battles. Hundreds were wounded or lost their lives on foreign battlefields. Many were recognized as talented and capable soldiers and at least fifty were awarded medals for bravery and heroism.

In addition to their contributing to the war effort by sending soldiers, many Indigenous communities and individuals made generous monetary donations to various war funds, and several communities established their own branch of the Red Cross and patriotic leagues.

REASONS FOR ENLISTING

There were various reasons that Indigenous people enlisted, including: the attraction of a regular wage, joining their family or friends who had enlisted, to satisfy their sense of adventure, to travel the world, and patriotism. Another reason for enlistment was to honour the past relationship between Aboriginal people and the British Crown during the war of 1812.

INDIGENOUS WOMEN IN WORLD WAR I

It was common for Indigenous women to remain on the home front to look after their homes and communities, raise children, or tend to family farms while the men were away. Indigenous women made their contributions on the home front in the form of charitable activities through the Red Cross and patriotic societies. The first Indigenous women's patriotic organization was the Six Nations Women's Patriotic League (SNWPL) formed on-reserve in Ontario in October 1914.

- These organizations contributed to the war effort by providing comforts to the soldiers such as knitted socks, sweaters, mufflers, and bandages.
- Young girls made these kinds of items to send to soldiers.
- They also collected clothing, money, and food to be sent overseas.

Indigenous women could not take advantage of the advancement of women's rights which occurred during the war period. They were not allowed to vote without loss of status until 1960. The sole exception was Charlotte Edith Anderson Monture, an Indigenous woman who served as a nurse during World War I, because she was an active member of the military.

CHARLOTTE EDITH ANDERSON MONTURE

Charlotte Edith Anderson Monture, a.k.a. Edith Monture, was one of fourteen Canadian Indigenous women who served as members of the Army Nurse Corps during World War I. She was born on April 10, 1890, on the Six Nations reserve near Brantford, Ontario, and died on April 3, 1996, in Oshwé:ken, Ontario.

As most Canadian nursing programs at the time excluded Indigenous women, Edith had no luck getting into Ontario nursing schools. The Canadian Indian Act was a barrier to higher education for Indigenous people, so Edith looked to the U.S., where she was accepted into New York's New Rochelle nursing school. She graduated first in her class.

Edith was the first Indigenous women to become a registered nurse in Canada and to gain the right to vote in a Canadian federal election. She was also the first Indigenous woman from Canada to serve in the United States military, breaking barriers for Indigenous women in the armed forces.

AFTER THE WAR

After returning from service, many Indigenous veterans were not awarded the same benefits as their non-Indigenous counterparts. Indigenous veterans returned with illnesses such as pneumonia, tuberculosis, and influenza. "Because mustard gas weakened the lungs, returning Indigenous soldiers who had been victims of gas attacks were more susceptible to contracting tuberculosis and other respiratory illnesses." Many unknowingly carried the deadly influenza virus back with them to their isolated communities, where it quickly spread. Sadly, many veterans returned home injured or missing limbs, which impacted their ability to provide for their families and communities.

More info:

- Canadian First Nations Influenza during WWI: ojs.library.ubc.ca/index.php/bcstudies/article/download/1498/1541/

- Post-war info: www.thecanadianencyclopedia.ca/en/article/indigenous-peoples-and-the-world-wars

RECOGNITION FROM THE CANADIAN GOVERNMENT

The equal treatment Indigenous veterans experienced while serving disappeared once they returned home to Canada. Veterans' benefits and support from the Canadian government were put in place, but the implementation of the programs on reserves was vastly different than elsewhere in Canada.

Receiving military decorations and commendations provided many with the confidence to speak for themselves and advocate for expanded rights and fair treatment in society for all members of their communities. Consequently, following the war, Indigenous people began to organize politically, with veterans leading the way. In 1919, the first national "pan-Indian" organization, the League of Indians in Canada, was founded by Lieutenant F.O. Loft, a Six Nations veteran.

MEDALS AND BARS

The Military Medal was first instituted on March 25, 1916, during World War I, to recognize bravery in battle. It was award to non-commissioned officers. The Military Medal was the equivalent to the Military Cross, which was awarded to commissioned officers.

A medal bar or medal clasp is a thin metal bar attached to the ribbon of a military decoration, civil decoration, or other medal. When used in conjunction with decorations for exceptional service, such as gallantry medals, the term "and bar" means that the award has been bestowed multiple times.

SPANISH FLU: 1918-1920

In the fall of 1918, a world ravaged by four years of war was suddenly hit by a mysterious and deadly plague – the "Spanish flu." The illness struck not only the young and the elderly, but also people in the prime of their lives, advancing rapidly toward mortality in its victims. This phenomenon brought the terror, the panic, the horror, and the sense of helplessness of the Great War home with the returning soldiers – more people died of this epidemic than had been killed in battle throughout the armed conflict.

Canada was hit hard by the illness. The spread of the infection included urban areas and even the most remote communities. Canada had a population of about 8.7 million in 1918, based on data from the 1921 census, and the death rate from Spanish flu totalled about 4.5 percent of the population. More than one thousand people died in Toronto alone, with a total of 8,700 deaths in Ontario. There were four thousand deaths in both Alberta and Manitoba and five thousand in Saskatchewan. Some Indigenous communities lost almost their entire populations to the illness. Most Canadian communities adopted measures to attempt to contain the spread of the virus. In Alberta people were required to wear face masks in public. In Regina people could be fined for coughing or sneezing in public. Some towns imposed quarantines, and people could not enter or leave without being arrested. Trains were forbidden to stop, and the borders were sealed and mail from overseas, feared to be carrying the deadly virus, was gathered and burned. In response to Spanish flu, Canada established the Department of Health in 1919.

More info:

- www.pc.gc.ca/en/culture/clmhc-hsmbc/res/doc/information
-backgrounder/espagnole-spanish

- www.thestar.com/life/health_wellness/2008/09/19/spanish
_flu_killed_millions_but_few_remember.html

PLAY-RELATED ACTIVITIES

BEFORE READING THE PLAY

Pictures from the Play

In a small group, look at the pictures of the play on pages 4, 42, and 59.

- Who could these people be?
- What can you tell from their outfits?
- What do you think their relationships are? (Do they seem friendly to each other? Do you think they are schoolmates?)
- What looks familiar to you? ·
- In which way are you able to identify with them?

Play with Words

In a small group, consider these topics mentioned in the play. What comes to mind when you hear those words? Try to come up with three examples and discuss with your group.

- WWI
- Pineapples
- First Nations
- Indian
- Vimy Ridge
- Grandparents
- Soldier
- Drama Queen
- It-Girl

AFTER READING THE PLAY

Class Conversations about the Play

Talk in class about the show you have just watched. Here are some questions to start the conversation:

- What are your thoughts about the play?
- What did you learn?
- What are you going to remember?
- Who was your favourite character and why?
- Did you recognize yourself in a character? In which way did you identify with them?
- Why do you think Peg called herself "Iron Peggy" at the end of the play?
- If you were the playwright, would you change anything in the story and why?

Operation "Stand Up"

Consider this quote in class: "They fought so we could be who we are meant to be. We have to stand up for who we are, and for those that came before us. We have to stand up for each other. It's something worth fighting for."

- What do you think this means?
- What are they fighting for?
- Is this relevant to you, your family, your community today? Why?
- Is Peg heroic?

- If settler colonialism is about replacing one society with another, can you identify any ways and in which countries this process may still be happening today? Discuss with a partner or in small groups.

Indigenous Communities

Research and discuss these questions with your class.

- What is the nearest Indigenous community to you?
- What do you know about their culture and traditions?
- How do they say "Hello" and "Goodbye"?
- What Traditional Regalia do they use for their Ceremonies? Can you draw an example?
- What is their most recognized form of artistic expression (mask, totem pole, dance, Oral History …)?
- Do they have a traditional set of colours?
- Do some research to find out about their participation in WWI.
- What do you know about your own ancestry?
- Where did your parents come from? Where did their parents come from?

Nani-Ma's Village

Peg's Grandma, or Nani-Ma, comes from North Delhi, which is a district just outside of New Delhi. North Delhi is bounded by the Yamuna River on the east, and by the districts of North West Delhi to the north and west, West Delhi to the southwest, Central Delhi to the south, and North East Delhi to the east across the Yamuna.

North Delhi has a population of 779,788 (2001 census), and an area of 59 km², with a population density of 13,019 people per km². North Delhi is inhabited by a wide range of people, jats (farmers) in particular – there are more than ninety villages inhabited by these farmers in the district.

In the play, Peg makes a model of her grandma's house. Do some research and create a model of what your grandparents' house looked like. It can be a real model or an electronic model.

A Letter for Grandma

In the play there are letters between Peg and her grandmother. Write a letter to your parents or grandparents on one of the following topics:

- What you've been doing lately at school
- Why they are special
- The most recent thing they helped you with
- Your favourite memories together

Peggy's Medals

Francis "Peggy" Pegahmagabow's medal set includes the Military Medal, with two bars, the 1914–15 Star, the British War Medal 1914–20, and the Victory Medal 1914–19. Pegahmagabow was Canada's most decorated Indigenous soldier in World War I. Peggy, as his fellow soldiers called him, enlisted in August 1914 and went overseas with the First Contingent. He served for most of the war as a scout and sniper with the 1st Battalion, acquiring a fearsome reputation as a marksman. At the Battle of Mount Sorrel in June 1916, Pegahmagabow captured a large number of German prisoners and was awarded the Military Medal. He was awarded a bar to his Military Medal during the Battle of Passchendaele in November 1917, and a second bar for actions during the Battle of Amiens in August 1918.

Medal set of Corporal Francis Pegahmagabow, M.M.**, CWM 20040035-001, Tilston Memorial Collection of Canadian Military Medals, Canadian War Museum.

Taran Kootenhayoo, Deneh'Cho Thompson, Adele Noronha, and Raes Calvert in *Iron Peggy*. Photo by Farah Nosh.

The soldiers in the play have all participated in WWI. They are famous soldiers who have been decorated with medals. Discuss the following questions in a small group.

- Do you know the significance of the medals?

- Do you know of anybody who has participated in WWI or in a more recent war? Perhaps your grandparents or great-grandparents.

- Do you know a story about the war?

- Why is it important to decorate soldiers?

- Each year on November 11, people around the world commemorate the end of WWI. Why is this important?

The Chant in the Play

Peg and the soldiers say this chant multiple times: "Still your mind. Steel your gut. Open your heart. Still your mind. Steel your gut. Open your heart."

- What is the message of the chant? What does it mean?
- What feelings are hidden in the chant?
- In which way is it an important message?
- Do you have a favourite object, poem, song, hero, or person that gives you strength and comfort when you need it?

Write your own chant:

1. that gives you strength to overcome an obstacle (mental or physical), or
2. that is your own reflection on the play, or
3. that is an acrostic chant to spell the title of the play (Iron Peggy). An acrostic is a poem in which the first letter of each line spells out a word, message, or the alphabet.

Anti-Bullying

Peg is bullied in the play. Bullying is not cool! It hurts people. Start a conversation with your class about how to prevent bullying with the following questions:

- What is being done at your school to prevent bullying?
- What can you do to help a person who is being bullied?
- Why do so many people not respond when they see someone getting bullied?

Prevent Bullying

Brainstorm with your class about steps you can take to prevent bullying. **Make it a code of conduct:** print it, sign it, and post it on your wall.

Kindness Rocks

Make "kindness rocks." Students can paint a rock and put their name or a message on it.

Send a Kind Note

Peg gets notes from her bullies. These notes have unkind words written on them. We need to be nice to each other and show appreciation!

1. Every person in the group needs to take a piece of paper.

2. Write your name at the bottom.

3. Pass it to the person next to you.

4. Write a short sentence AT THE TOP of the page to show your appreciation of the person whose name is written at the bottom of the page.

5. Fold the paper over to hide the sentence you just wrote.

6. Pass the paper to the person next to you.

7. Repeat step four to six until the whole page is folded multiple times with compliments.

8. Once everyone has had the chance to write a compliment return the paper back to its original owner.

Write a Review

Write a review of the play! Be honest and write down your thoughts. What did you think of it? Did you like it? Would you recommend it to other people?

Review Title:

Stars: ☆ ☆ ☆ ☆ ☆

Intro (Important facts: who, when, where …):

Middle (What happens during the play?):

End (Conclusion, what is the message?):

The publisher has made a concerted effort to contact the relatives of Francis Pegahmagabow, George McLean, and Edith Monture for permission to reproduce their images. We ask anyone with information relating to their families to contact us.

PHOTO: EMILY COOPER

Marie Clements is an award-winning Métis/Dene writer, director, and producer who ignited her brand of artistry in a variety of mediums including theatre, film, television, and radio. Of late, Marie's play *The Unnatural and Accidental Women* opened the first national Indigenous theatre at the National Arts Centre in Ottawa last fall, her opera *Missing*, produced by Pacific Opera, toured nationally, her play *Burning Vision* was produced by the National Theatre School in Montréal, and her commissioned play *Iron Peggy* premiered at the Vancouver International Children's Festival. Marie's fifteen plays have been presented on some of the most prestigious stages, garnering numerous awards and publications, including the Canada-Japan Literary Award, and two Governor General's Literary Award nominations. Marie's multi-award-winning films have screened internationally at Cannes, TIFF, MOMA, VIFF, AIFF, and the ImagineNATIVE Film Festival. Her recent film credits include the dramatic feature *Red Snow*, music documentary *The Road Forward*, and *Looking at Edward Curtis*. Marie is the founder of Urban Ink Productions, artistic director of Red Diva Projects, and president of her media production company, MCM.